Butlins Wonder West in Ayr

Debbie Ross

DEDICATION

There can be only one – Jane Walker - what were we like – we lived in our own little bubble – we lived in each other's pockets - there was never any doubt in my mind about our friendship from day one. From the first minute I saw you until this day – We have been on some journey together from then until now and you will always be in my life. I love you – I have never told you, but I do, and god knows what we will get up to next.

To all the parties that took place in the chalets

To all the crazy nights in the Beachcomber

To all the Cowboying of tables

To the smashing of plates and fighting with the Chefs

To all the sex drugs and Rock in Roll

To the free booze

To all the stolen pictures from the shop

To all the free rides at the shows

To all the free shots on the Go Karts

To getting chapped up for work every morning

To turning up to work either drunk or speed bombs

To the worst bloody uniform ever

To all the friendships that we made

To Butlins Wonder West World in Ayr

Butlin's
H LIDAY
WORLDS

Butlin's
HOLIDAY
WORLDS
— and —
HOTELS

Ref: AMD/LB

...applicant,

...MENT AT WONDERWEST WORLD

...to the recent telephone conversation with a member ...from this Office concerning employment at Wonderwest

...confirm that you have been offered employment as

...RESS......

...tion is offered on a live-in basis and you should ...the Personnel Department at Wonderwest World no ...3.00 p.m. on Friday 10th May, 1991.

...ing this letter as confirmation of your appointment ...ble you to gain access to the Centre.

...erely,

...orans
...& Training Executive

ACKNOWLEDGMENTS

Special thanks to Donna Shannon who found us and reunited us all

Jane Walker, Donna Shannon, Allison Knox, Caroline McDonald, Betty Barr, Jim Patterson, Chris Dawson, Lorraine Fraser, George Hall, Hugh Brown, Joseph Scott, Marie McCrum, Liz Murray, Jim Jack, Tony Clarke, Paul Burke, Colin Scougall, Lorraine Fraser, Carol Anne Mooney, Susan Glancy, Eddie McGrath, James Livingston, Jim Medowcroft, James Livingston, Jane Robertson, Kevin Boyle, & Paul Burke

And to everyone who ever worked there – I did tell people I was writing a book and if anyone wanted to add their own experience and some people have - they are in their own words

I hope I have done it Justice

Chapter 1

Jesus fucken Christ will you stop moaning. I am nearly ready; my dad is bursting my ball. I am one of those people who will be late for her own funeral. My dad is the total opposite that idiot would be lined up in the coffin waiting to die. I am just about to go for an interview there was an advert in the paper for staff at Butlins in Ayr. They were looking for Red Coats, Waitresses, Bar staff the whole shebang. People to cover all positions within the complex. It was live in position for everyone and they were paying £62.05 weekly. Now this is going back 30 years when Butlins was actually Butlins and not Haven or whatever shit they call it now. We were the real Butlins. The all singing and dancing proper Butlins before it became shit. I wanted to be a waitress. I knew that if I got the waitress position, I would make more money. Waitresses get tips. I was working in Bonkers in the city center which funnily enough is not Bonkers anymore. I was making a packet. I was up dancing on the bar in my pink and yellow socks giving it big licks in between serving customers. I was the best waitress in there. I made the most money on tips I made a shit load of money. Now I knew if I could just get the waitress position I would be laughing. I can talk the legs off a donkey and sell sand to an Arab, telling him it is magical sand. I will say anything to get a sale or a tip. If you support Celtic so do I, if you sleep in bed with a teddy then so do I. If you take it up the arse, then so do I. I knew if I got the waitress position, I would be quid's in. I have a bubbly personality so I know I will make good tips. Now all I need to do is get the job.

I wish I had got the bloody bus; all he has done is moan from the minute we got in the car. He moans I am never ready in time; he moans I will never get a job if I do not turn up on time, he moans about moaning. Thank fuck he is not the one giving me the interview, or I would never get the bastard job. It will be moaning all the way home if I do not get the job. I am dying to get away from home. I am eighteen now and I share a room with my sister. It is not as if I have anything to hide, I just want my own space. I hate sharing a room. I hate being at home and I want to experience as much as I possibly can.

Now he starts with the questions. What are you going to say if they ask this, what are you going to say if they ask that? What will you say if they ask where will you be in five years' time? I have never got this question. Whoever made that question up for interviews must have been one thick bastard. If you knew where you were going to be in five years' time you would be in the bookies placing bets. The lottery was not around thirty years ago. It is the most stupid question ever. Yet everybody asks it, does that mean everybody is thick or they are just stupid. Or they do not know what else to ask. You know within a few minutes of someone walking through the door if you are going to give them the job or not. It is how you bond and interact with the person. If anyone says different, they are full of shit. No matter how many qualifications you have if you walk through that door and act like a dick you are not getting the job. Or the person interviewing might have a stick stuck up their arse, if you talk like me you are

fucked. You are not getting the job. You know the minute you walk in that door what the interviewer is like and act accordingly. If your face fits you are getting the job, if not cheerio.

When we got there, it did not look like anything. There was a small like cabin box at the front and a big billboard with Butlins Wonder west World. Now I saw the pictures at home, there was a beach, shows, loads of shops, amusements swimming etc. and all I see is a billboard, a box and hedges. As we drive up a man comes to the car and asks for your pass. I had my interview letter, so he lets us in and told us just to follow the road down to the main reception. As you start to drive in that is when you see everything. It looks like nothing from outside but as you get passed the gate bit it is huge. I remember thinking I had never seen anything as big as this in my life. We could see the building that the swimming was in because you could see part of the chutes and part of the building was all glass so you could see inside the swimming. There were shops and amusements, I could see a big wheel in the distance. People were just crossing the road in front of the car as if it were not even there. It just looked busy. We found the main reception and in I went with my letter. They were holding the interviews in the dining hall. They did not even show you where to go it was a case of if you go outside walk along and it is the big building on the left. Then a look of make your own way there because I am too fucken lazy to get up and show you where it is.

The dining hall was massive. Jesus Christ the whole of Noah's ark could have a field day in it. There were so many tables and chairs, but it did not look overcrowded. They were all spaced out with loads of room between each table. It was not like a restaurant where you sit at a table and you can hear what the people in the next table are saying. You would need a microphone for that. It was just massive. I do not know what other words to use other than massive. So, in the huge room there was an eight-seater table and that is where the managers were sitting. It looked stupid. It did look like a needle in a haystack.

The lady who was interviewing me her name was Joan. She had short dark hair, about a size 10 and she had a pretty face. She did not have any makeup on, and she did not need makeup. She was naturally pretty. She was quite softly spoken. There was an assistant manageress beside her with long blonde hair, she was naturally pretty too, she had a nose ring in, and her name was Sammy. As I started talking to them, they saw my bubbly personality, and they asked me to be a Red Coat. Fuck that I am not being a bastard Red Coat they work all day and night with kids for no tips, and so I lied. I said that I was ok around adults, but I am no good around kids. I can talk to adults all day long, but I fear kids. The main thing of being a Red Coat was to entertain the kids and their parents. I knew that their shifts started at the crack of dawn and they are last to finish. That would have been the job from hell for me. Kids annoy me I would be a shit Red Coat, even though it is more money and it is the job everyone wants I know I will make more money being a waitress. The only job I wanted was to be a waitress. I talked them out of giving me the position of Red Coat into a waitress. My start date was 21st April 1991.

Chapter 2

I know I am going to be away all season. I do have friends at home, but I need to get away. If you have read growing up in Sighthill you will understand why I need to go. I am not going to get into it in this book so if you have not read it then I will not spoil it but just know I need to leave.

I have friends that I have hung about with for years, I know I am going to miss them, but it is the better alternative. You say your goodbyes and I am one of these people who cannot cry. Am I sad when Bambi dies, yes of course I am I am human, but I just cannot cry? It takes a lot for me to cry. As I say cheerio to my friends before I go some of them are crying and I spit on my hand and wipe it in my eye. I do not want to seem as if I did not give a fuck but the reason, I had to go was the only thing that would make me cry and I could not do it in front of him. Of course, it had to be a boy. It always is, it is just complicated so we will fast forward.

Saying goodbye to my family was a cheerio see you later. Do not phone me I will phone you kind of thing. They are my family, but we are not close let us just say that. I was happy to leave and they were happy that I was leaving. I was a nightmare growing up. I rebelled a lot where my sister never. She was little miss goodie two shoes and I was the wicked daughter. The daughter who caused no end of grief. I would stay out all night and do all-nighters in the streets with my friends. Now when I think back, I think what a fucken tube I was. I chose to stay out on the cold streets all night or on the stairs of the high flats playing Prisoner Cell Block H with my pal Kenny and all he went on about all night was the fucken texture of the walls. Yes, we were drunk, but I chose to either walk about the cold streets all night or on cold stairs rather than in my bed. I would tell my mum and dad I was staying with Lynne; she would say the same to her parents and a group of us would do all-nighters. Fucken idiots. Imagine trying to get the kids these days to do that. They would have heart palpitations if they are without Wi-Fi for 20 minutes never mind all night but that is what you did back in those days. You were part of the "in crowd" if you stayed out on the streets all night.

I remember one weekend my wee cousin Elaine was staying with me for the weekend. My mum told me to be home for 10pm Like that was going to happen, we stayed out until after 12am. Anything my mum told me to do I would do the complete opposite. We came home and my mum had locked the fucken door. We were staying in the high flats at the time. On every landing they used to have a drying cupboard. It was like a cupboard door and when you opened it, it had metal rods and they heated up to dry your clothes. It did dry your clothes, but they were stiff as fuck because it was dry heat. The towels were like sandpaper if you put them in there. You would come out the bath all nice and smelling wonderful and use a fucken towel and you were all red because it was like rubbing sandpaper all over your skin. The point is we had to spend the night up against the door in the landing because she locked us out. We put the drying cupboard on to get a heat.

Elaine was staying the next night also. My mother said if we were not back by 10pm then she would lock us out again as if that would make me go home at 10pm. Did it fuck, we just did not go home that night. We stayed out all night. There were a few of us it was a great laugh. We were having a wonderful time until it started pissing of rain and we had nowhere to go. We were in

Ballornock that night. They did not have high flats that we could have gone into to get away from the rain. One of the guys said he knew someone who would let us crash with them for the night. It was the middle of the night early hours of the next morning, but he said that they would still be awake so off we popped.

We got to the house and he forgot to tell us that they were druggies. Now I do not care what the fuck you do or what you do to get your kicks. We have all been there with recreational drugs, but it was heroin. They were shooting up right in front of us and I thought fuck that I am sleeping with one eye open. We would have been better off sleeping on the landing again. I am in panic mode and Elaine thinks this is the best night ever. She has pulled a guy; she is staying out all night having the time of her life. I am thinking are we going to wake up in the middle of the night with them trying to put drugs in us. I never slept that night. I lay in a bed with my eyes open. Elaine was out for the count. We were all in a room with 2 double beds. I was going out with a guy called Der at the time. Us two were in one bed and Elaine and Garry were in the other bed and they started having fucken sex in the same room. We were two foot away from them if you were lucky and we heard everything. Now when I think back it sounds stupid as fuck but back then it was not. I could have been in my own bed and had a great sleep instead I am in some druggy's house lying with my eyes open just wanting to go home.

The following morning, we were all up at the swing park and I saw my dad's car, oh fuck this is not good. He went mental everybody was at the swing park all the people we hung about with and my dad kicks off. My mum is worried we never came home bla de bla. Too fucken right we never came home. She said she was going to lock us out again. So, she must have known the night before that we did come back, and she left us in the landing to teach us a lesson that clearly backfired. Now we were in the shit, my mum had even phoned my aunty Rena and grassed Elaine in and then we are both in the shit.

That was pretty much the way my teenage years went. Trying to stay away from the house as much as I could. Going to Butlins was going to be a bittersweet. I would get away from the house, but I was losing the love of my life.

Chapter 3

I have arrived with everything except the fucken kitchen sink. My dad's car is full to maximum capacity. My mum and sister cannot come in the car I have that much shit. This is where I am going to be living for the next God knows how long so anything that was mine has come with me. The kitchen sink just did not come off the wall or I would have taken that too. I get into the reception bit and they give you all this paperwork to sign and go over conditions bla bla bla. I tell my dad that he can go now. I do not want to be seen with one of my parents. I am an adult now. I am going to be looking after myself. Just you go and I will get all the paperwork etc. done.

I got my staff pass, we had already provided photos for this, you get the terms and conditions of your position, the terms and conditions of your Chalet, we were all live in. That came part and parcel of the position. Even although it was only an hour or so up the road the positions were still live in. Especially the waitresses as they had to do morning breakfast. Well our shifts were split into 2 separate bits. The morning breakfast, and then night-time dinner. It would be impossible for a waitress to go home after doing the breakfast and then back in time for dinner. After serving the breakfast and clearing up you then had to reset the tables for dinner time, so we all lived in. Our meals are included every day, breakfast, lunch and dinner but we eat in a separate building from where we serve the meals to holiday people. Basically, that is it they said, here is your key to your Chalet and just walk around yourself to find your bearings and enjoy. Your first shift starts at 7am. You need to go and collect your uniform and if you wanted a TV for your room it was £5 a week to rent it.

Now I am an arsehole, why did I tell my dad to go when I have all these fucken bags. I had my bedroom in bags. They do not give you help like they do in a hotel with your luggage, it is a fucken job. Take your own shit to your Chalet. I took two bags at first just until I found out where I was living and then I would go back for the other bags. Fuck me, it was miles away. It is staff Chalets so there is no way they are going to be near the reception. Not a fucken chance they are miles away. This guy is showing me where I go. I am five-foot fuck all. I have wee legs. This guy is about 6 feet and looks like Herman Munster. He takes one step and I need to take three to catch him up. He is just strolling along, and I am like a Duracell bunny on speed trying to catch up. He is not even looking behind to see if I am there. He does not give a fuck. I have taken him away from his cushy number on the reception and now he must show me where to go. If he starts speed walking, then I am totally fucked because I cannot sprint, and I have two heavy ass bags that he has not even offered to take one. Yeah mate fuck you, I hope I am serving your food because it will get a big groger in it and I will take it from the back of my throat for good measure. Fuck you. Eventually we got to the lane of the Chalets. The staff Chalets are miles away. It is like keep the riff raff at bay. The Red Coats Chalets were closer to the complex. The Red Coat that I talked myself out of the job. It was every other staff member chalet before ours the waitresses and chefs were last. We were the scum of the staff. They did not put baby in the corner they put her in the middle of nowhere. He did not even walk me down to show me which one was mine. He simply put his hand out and said that row there number 13.

That is exactly what they looked like a row. See if you get council flats that are in a row with a staircase to flats above this is what it looked like. The row went on for miles. It was just a row of doors and numbers but there were sets of stairs after say every 10 or so doors and they took you to another level. The girls were on the ground level the boys were upstairs. It did not look like anything fancy. The red coats had the better Chalets. We got the dregs, but I love the dregs. I just hope I am going to like my roommate because it was two people to a Chalet.

When I found my room and opened it there was no one in. It was the basic of basics. It was like a room for a nun. As soon as you opened the door there was like an old-style brown wardrobe. A twin size one. Two like camp size beds. One at each end of the wardrobe and at the bottom on one bed was a set of brown drawers. To the left was a small bathroom with a toilet and a bath. There was not enough room to swing a cat in here and I have a shit load of bags. It looks like two people need to share one wardrobe and one set of drawers. I would be as well throwing everything away because it sure as fuck is not going to fit in here. I put my bags down and had a pee then I tried to find my way back to the reception to get the rest of my stuff.

Four bloody trips it took. Not one person said they would help. No men, no women no anyone. Everyone was just getting on with what they were doing, and it was as if I was invisible walking along with my bags. Or should I say struggling along with my bags. The bags were bigger than me. It was like carrying two extra people about each trip. By the time I was finished I was fucked. I had no energy left to go and look about. I used it all up carrying the bags for miles. I bloody better like this job because I am not carrying all that stuff back again. Me and my big bloody mouth. Oh, dad you just go. When I was doing one of my many trips, I would see people with their parents, and they were helping them with their bags. I was just too much in a hurry to be a grown up. I shot

myself in the foot. Yeah dad you just go. You just go and I will carry the bags myself.

I was totally fucked but I still wanted to go out and see what was what. At least this time I would not have to carry the bags about just myself. I had already seen everything from the reception to the Chalet, but I wanted to see everything. My roommate was still not in, so I left my stuff without unpacking and off I went.

The place was massive. As I was walking from the reception to my chalet, I saw this big building, but I did not see what it was inside. I could see part of stage and there was another building behind that. It was huge, I do not know what other words to say or use other than it was huge. As I walked about one of the buildings was called The Showboat this was for adults. They had another huge building called Harlequins which was for family's entertainment with a bar and huge dance floor, there were so many different buildings and bars. It was too much to take in on one afternoon after carrying all they bags but it was amazing. There were hot food places, amusements, shops, more buildings. More shops and this was just one part. The bit where all the caravans were had a huge fun fair. Go karting. Swimming with huge chutes. It was massive there was something for everyone. They catered for kids, adults, bingo, family entertainment, adult entertainment, shows and much more. There was something for everyone all the time. It was nonstop entertainment from sun rise to sun set. I just knew I was going to have the time of my life.

Chapter 4

I have just met my roommate and I have taken a sudden dislike to her. Do not ask me why but instantly I did not like her. She is like me. She has red hair, hers is long though and she has a poodle perm. Remember they perms you used to get way back and you were a walking advert for a tight ass poodle. Well this is how her hair looked. She was the same height as me. Five-foot fuck all. She had freckles and I hate to say but she was not an attractive woman. If you have read any of my other stories you will know I will say women are attractive if I think they are. I give credit where credit is due, but she got skelpt with the ugly branches of the tree. It was a fact. No amount of makeup was going to make this girl look beautiful. Her name was Charlie, even a line of Charlie would not make her good looking. The point is I took an instant dislike to her and I had to live with her. She had been here the year before. This was her second season and she thought she was the bee's knees. See they people you get if you give them a badge or something and the power goes to their heads. This is how she was; her badge was it was her second season and she knew everything about everything, and she would say so. I do not know if that was what put me off her. I just do not know; I just know I did not like her and yet I had to live with her.

She did not shut up the whole night. She went on about this that and the next thing and I felt cheated. I felt cheated out of seeing and experiencing things for myself. Kind of like someone gives you a wrapped present and you cannot wait to see what is inside and some fucker goes and spoils it for you by telling you what is inside before you open it. This is how I felt, she ruined the unwrapping for me her and her big bloody mouth. As we both lay there on our beds, she was busy telling me about how everything worked, and I lay there imagining smashing her face off one of the machines.

Chapter 5

It is my first day of work. This is going to be my first experience in the dining hall even though motor mouth spoiled most of it for me last night I was excited. I was excited to meet new friends because I knew as sure as I know my own name that Charlie would not be in my circle of friends in fact I knew within the first five minutes of meeting her I was going to get a swap as fast as I could and I would do whatever it took to get the swap. I was not going to let her spoil it for me. I just nodded and said yes in the morning until I got out the fucken door away from her. I am one of these people who will be late for my own funeral, yet I am up and away and will be at work early just to get her to fuck. I am fed up listening to her. If she were advertising jobs for the place there would be no staff. She was a mixture of a boring ass C***(I hate that word) and a moaning face get. It was all she did all night. She moaned or complained about everything and I thought to myself why the fuck have you come back then. She was a waitress as well I am sure to God; she never made any tips. They would pay for her not to be their waitress for the week. I felt sorry for whoever got lumbered with her for the week. I would have asked for my money back or to move tables. Whoever you got on the Monday was with you all week to Friday and then there were the weekenders who only came on a Saturday and Sunday. If you only had to put up with her for two days, it might not be so bad but five fucken days would be hell. I knew within five minutes I did not like her.

As soon as I got into the dining hall, I ditched her, it was enormous this could have held well over 2000 people and still have plenty room. It was huge. The tables were already set up. Everyone was starting the same day except motor mouth. The people who had been there last year started a few days before us to get the place ready. It was like see the tables you get in school dinners the big long ones. Well this is what it was like the tables would sit twelve people to a table, so it was either one big ass family or a few families put together. You wanted it to be a few families put together, so you got more tips. They were all set up with the nice crisp white tablecloths, cutlery, plates and napkins. I had to admit it did look awesome. I had never seen anything so big in my life.

The manageress Joan shouted us all to the front of the dining room to go over everything with us. I felt like saying there is no point because motor mouth already ruined it for me. As we all came to the front together my eye caught this girl. Out of all the people in the hall this one girl caught my eye. She was the same height as me she had long blonde hair a cute innocent little face, she reminded me of Sandy in Greece. Remember when she was boring plain Sandy before she turned into a hot ass chick at the end. Well this is exactly how she looked. Why was I attracted to her then because I am more like a boy? I do not really get on with girls, yet this cute little quiet thing has caught my eye, so I go and stand next to her and introduce myself as Demi. It only turns out that we stay 10 minutes away from each other at home. As soon as she opened her mouth to tell me her name was Jenna and where she was from the nice cute innocent Sandy left as quick as she came. She was a fowl mouthed midget like me. I knew instantly that we would be brilliant friends.

We were at the dining room for 7am. Joan went over what would happen and where we get the food etc. from. The tables were already set up to give us a head start but also to show you how they wanted the tables to look when they were set up. She showed us where to get stuff in the dining room and then she was

taking us into the kitchen. Oh my mother of god see as soon as the doors were opened from the dining hall into the kitchen all you could hear was fuck this, fuck that, fuck you, fucken move, fuck, fuck and more fucks. I wondered then when they were asking for chefs if they put in the advert you must be able to say fuck because it is all you heard the minute that door opened. The kitchen was enormous I guess it had to be because well over 2000 people could get fed at any one given time. Everything was sparkling clean, silver and shiny. There were so many chefs all running about in white uniforms and white hats shouting fuck. This was all you heard. Now I know I swear but without exaggerating you are lucky if you got on normal word and then fuck. She showed us about the kitchen and where to get the food and plates from meanwhile all these chefs are carrying on doing what they are doing and shouting. You would have thought we were invisible because they did not even acknowledge that we were there. They were too busy running about swearing at each other. After she showed us what was what in the kitchen, she took us back into the dining room and closed the door and you could not hear them. The minute the door was opened again then all you heard were all the chefs swearing.

The tables were already pre-set. This is how they wanted the tables to look. After breakfast they would show us how to set the tables up for dinner time. This is when it was all out war. When you finished clearing away the breakfast dishes and setting up for the night-time dinner it was mayhem. Everybody was stealing stuff off of each other's tables. We called this cowboying tables. If some people did not turn up for breakfast you had spare cutlery etc. but your tables had to be set for the next sitting before you could leave. This meant waiting for clean dishes to reset your table. If you were clever though you would steal stuff off other people's tables when they were not looking so you did not need to wait for clean dishes. Everyone did it so it was mayhem you did not want to leave your tables and go into the kitchen because the minute your back was turned your fucken dishes went. I had already heard about this from Charlie but hearing it and seeing it are two different things. The lengths people would go to, to get clean dishes. I used to hide mine in the plant pots or under the tables on a chair but then everyone started doing it. People would find the weirdest of places to hide stuff or go to mental lengths to pinch other people's stuff. This was a big deal in our department. If you asked 100 people what the main thing was about the dining hall and all 100 would come back and say cowboying tables. Even all the other staff knew what cowboying tables were. As in the Red coats, shop staff, bar staff anyone and everyone knew about cowboying tables. If your tables were not set for nighttime or breakfast you would need to go up earlier to get your tables ready. If you were clever like me and Jenna if we did not have our tables ready, we would pay a guy called Aldo to go and set our tables up for us.

The first shift was totally nuts when the holiday makers came in and we sat them at their tables the minute we went into the kitchen the chefs running about swearing who did not acknowledge us when we first went in to get shown about now acknowledged us but all they did was scream and shout at us and there were a shit load of fucks getting thrown about. It was absolute chaos. I for one do not like people telling me what to do never mind telling me what to do and putting about 6 fucks in one sentence. Hell no, they were shouting swearing at me, I did the same back. Jenna was wanting to rip their heads off and piss down their throat. I thought I was bad and to think I thought she looked like the nice boring Sandy before she became hot. She was a pocket rocket with a gun up her arse. She was giving it welly in the kitchen. I am sure at one point she was going to wrap the plate around the chef's face, and I was buckled. This tiny little five-foot fuck all was mouth almighty. I just knew we were going to be amazing friends. The rest of the morning went the same way. The chefs would shout at the waitresses and vice versa. I swear to god if the holiday makers could hear what was going on in the kitchen they would have bolted. Although the dining room held over 2000 people it seemed so quiet compared to the kitchen. Trust me a deaf person would hear something the kitchen was that bad. There were plates getting thrown about and people throwing cutlery at each other it was organised chaos and yet it worked.

Now when I think back if it had been a normal kitchen it would not have been right. The kitchen was part of the madness. I swear about 100 plates got smashed at every serving. The chefs threw plates at each other or the waitresses and they would throw them back. See if someone complained about the food the waitress would lob the plate and the contents at the chef. There were two servings every day and this went on at both servings. I loved it to you it might sound like all-out war, but it was just the way the kitchen worked. If you were a timid little mouse you would not survive one shift let alone one season. Charlie did not tell me this bit, and this was the best bit. A normal person would probably pack their shit and go. I loved it. I knew there and then this was going to be one of the best years of my life and so it was.

Chapter 6

Jenna and I fast became friends. I wanted her to be my Chalet mate, but she was already in a Chalet with a girl called Dee. Dee was the tallest out of the three of us. She was maybe 5 foot 5 or 6. She had dark hair; it was kind of permed. Not like Charlies fuck sake she was a walking advert for do not stick your finger in a plug socket because this is what will happen you are a poodle gone wrong. It was more natural curls. She was the same as me and Jenna she did not wear makeup. She did not need make up. She was naturally pretty, and she was a nice person so they two had a chalet together and I was still with Charlie. I needed to ditch Charlie I knew I would find a way to do it eventually. The sooner the better. I spent all my time in Jenna and Dee's chalet.

Dee had her own group of friends but either Jenna and I would do stuff together or me, Jenna, Dee and some of her friends but we were all always together at night in the Beachcomber. This is where everyone went at night. It was like a dancing type thing with a bar. The staff could drink in there but so were the holiday makers. They just did not allow kids in. This is where we hung about every night. It was brilliant. We always pimped Jenna out. I mean she was naturally pretty with the long blonde hair and she looks stunning. If she would just keep her gob shut then you would think she was Sandy, we would get her to go and become friends with all the men behind the bar in the Beachcomber so we could get free booze. We would just tell her not to go in all guns blazing, you look like Sandy can you please just act like Sandy until we get free drink. We did this to her in all the bars and clubs in Butlins. Basically, we pimped her out for free booze, but it worked. She would chat away to the guys and dangle a carrot at them. Let them think that it could go somewhere but really all we wanted was free booze.

One night in the Beachcomber Jenna asked me if I wanted a gram of speed. I had only ever tried it once before. It was just the two of us. We had now known each other a few weeks. We practically lived in each other's pockets. The only time I went to my chalet was to go to sleep. I still did not like Charlie. The longer it went on the more she would do my head in. Anything she said or did annoyed the life out of me. I kept hoping and wishing that she would get sacked and I could have the chalet to myself. Ok, I will do it. Let us take a gram of speed. Now remember we are up for breakfast serving every morning. Breakfast is at 8am so we need to be in the dining hall before that. The assistant manageress Sammy would come and chap all of our doors in the morning to make sure we were all up. You did not have mobile phones back then. Half of us were still drunk at 8am. They did not care, as long as you made it for your shift drunk or not you still managed to go. If we were hanging badly then I would serve my breakfast and then let my holiday makers hide me under the table. All they cared about was turning up for work. Drunk or sober it did not matter if you served the breakfast. You still had to reset your tables for night-time but the time in between I would be hiding under the table sleeping or under the table eating their food. We got all our meals provided but our food was not like the food we served to the holiday makers. We got cheap shite. Jenna and I never ate out of the staff dining hall we always had our breakfast and dinner with our holiday makers. We would give them an extra dinner and tell them to keep it for us. Once you had served everyone their meals we would hide under the tables and eat our breakfast and dinner.

We were up all night after the Beachcomber we went to Jenna

and Dee's chalet. We did not tell Dee what we had done she was well past drunk. We sat with Dee until she fell asleep because she was really bad and me and Jenna sat up all night talking shit. Jesus Christ the conversations we had were totally meaningless, but they seemed so important at the time. If you have never taken a gram of speed it is like you are a budgie and someone has locked you up since forever and this is your first time seeing or speaking to anyone and you cannot shut up. No matter how hard you try you cannot shut up. You chew the inside of your mouth. You cannot eat if you are pissed drunk it sobers you up. If you take speed and drink at the same time. You cannot get drunk. We sat and spoke seven shades of shite all night until the early morning. I went back to my chalet just before 7am because I knew Sammy would come and chap us all up at 7am for work. We did not need chapped up for work but we did not want Dee to know we had been up all night taking drugs either we looked as if we have been pulled through a hedge backwards and we started to get tired and then Jenna brings out more speed and says it will help us get through our shift.

Through our shift by fuck, I had only ever taken it once before last night. I have never taken it then taken it again the same day. Jesus fuck I could not shut up. I was being nice to the chefs. All my holiday makers were getting a full running commentary of what happened last night just minus the drugs part. I was even in the kitchen offering to help do the fucken dishes. All the chefs are still running about swearing like troopers and I am apologising to them whereas usually I am as bad as Jenna. I will throw plates and cutlery at the chefs. If they swear at me, I am swearing back but that morning I was being nice and offering to help. I did not care about cowboying people's tables that morning. I was offering to stay and do other people's tables and they could pay me back

when I was not speeding out my nut.

The breakfast serving was the shortest service. We were in and out and I still had all this energy and wanted to do something. We had been here for weeks and we had not seen past the pub. We went to the dinner hall to serve, our separate food hall to eat and the pub. We lived in the pub. So, when we finished doing the breakfast shift, we took a walk around to see what else there was. There was a row of gift shops that we had never been in and then we saw this other shop, but it had all photos in it. It was just a shop with rows and rows of photos. So off we go and there were pictures of me, Jenna and Dee. The photographer obviously does not know who staff is and who are the holiday makers when we are out of our uniform. They have photographers walking about the complex taking photos of holiday makers. There were other photographers at the fun fair, the various clubs. There were photographers everywhere taking pictures of people and putting them in the shop to sell them. I think there were about 5 or 6 pictures of us all and so we pinched them. I think it was about £3/£4 for a photo. We had our uniforms on the blouses had buttons all the way up and so we opened some of our buttons and put the photos in there and walked out. Everyone did this and if they say they did not do it and paid for them they are talking shit. They were all pictures of us in normal clothes. The uniforms were horrendous Jesus mother of God they were horrible. We had these blue skirts, they were not navy blue or light blue it was an in-between horrible blue, the blouses and shirts were yellow and white checks. They were hellish and we had a little apron thing at the front of the skirt which was the same colour as the blouse. Out of all the staff and uniforms ours was by far the worst. We made the most money, but the uniform was hideous. You would not be caught dead walking down the street in it. Some of the girls rolled their skirts up so they looked nice and short but they were that long you had to roll them up several times so yes they looked shorter but you looked as if you were a size 20 round the waist they were rolled up that many times. Some girls cut theirs and then sewed them up. People tried everything and anything to make them look wearable, but it was pointless they were totally hellish. As soon as the serving was over, we would go and get changed straight away.

We went in and out of all the shops. There was loads of them. Weeks we had been there not days weeks and we had seen saw fuck all except our chalets and the pub. The speed is still in full force so now we are actually going to take a walk around the place and see what there is. I know we should have done this from day one, but we were young and all we wanted to do was have some fun. We went back to our chalets and got changed to go a walk.

Dee did not make breakfast serving. We were all smashed last night but me and Jenna took a gram of speed. Dee was well past a gram of speed. A mountain of the stuff would not have set her straight. Someone thought that drinking straight vodka would be a great idea. Just vodka on vodka. We had to practically carry her back to the Chalet and we stopped every two minutes because she thought she was going to be sick. The walk between the Beachcomber and our chalets did not seem that far away but when you are trying to carry someone, and they want to stop every two minutes to spew. It felt as if it had taken us hours to get her back to the Chalet.

To be fair she did look bad. We knew she was not making work today. Jena and I were still rattling so we said that we would share her tables for breakfast and dinner, and she could sleep off the hangover. Everything was fine until she went onto straight vodka and Huey became her best friend last night along with the toilet pan. There would have been no point giving her any drugs. She would have spewed them, and I think she would have been much better off sleeping it off rather than staying up all night. Jenna offered her a gram of speed, she had never taken it before, and we told her that it would take her hangover away, but she just would not sleep. We were home to get changed anyway to go a walk about and see the place and what is here. She could take it and try it by the time we are ready she might be feeling better.

Took the hangover away? She was up and out that bed like Jack Flash rearing and ready to go. I swear to god see the difference it did not even take 20/30 minutes to kick in. It was as if it kicked in instantly and she wanted out. So off we all pop to go and have a wander about. Now our chalets were like level with what we called the main drag. This is where all the clubs, family entertainment, amusements, cafes and shops were but there was another huge part that we had not been to yet. You could see it in the distance, or should I say you could see the big wheel in the distance. The complex had an actual fare ground with a big dipper and things like that. We just had not been down to see it yet. As we made our way down there was a crazy golf bit, then that took you onto the go karts before you hit the shows. From far away it only looked as if there were a few things there but there was not it was a huge fare ground with all the mod con shows that you would get. Kind of like the Irn Bru carnival but on a smaller scale. It was all free. It was free for holiday makers because they paid for their weeks holiday and the entertainment comes part and package. The only thing that was not free was the go karts. We had to pay for the go karts but everything else was free and right on our doorstep. We could have gone to the fare every day all day

if we wanted to. It is like the old cliché you do not know what you have got until its gone. It was all literally on our doorstep and because it was, we never hardly used it. The only place we lived in was the Beachcomber and our Chalets. The world was our oyster and we chose drink over attractions.

Chapter 7

This speed thing has become a ritual for us. We are both now taking it every day. I cannot even say we take it as soon as we wake up because we are not even getting to bed. As soon as it starts to wear off and we begin to get tired then we are taking another speed bomb. I hate the taste of it. Even thinking about it makes me gag and Jenna makes me these speed bombs with fag papers. She wraps the speed up in a cigarette paper and twists it. It kind of looks like they things you used to throw, and they would bang. You used to get them in the joke shop. You would throw them on the ground, and they would make a snap noise. This is what a speed bomb looks like. It is supposed to help your teeth from rotting. That is another thing. You suck the top of your mouth like a dummy tit. I do not know why you do this, but you just do and bite the sides of your cheeks. The inside of my mouth is a bloody mess between bite marks and sucking the top of my mouth.

We have gone weeks without sleeping. We go to work in the morning, we either go into Ayr during the day for a wee while or hang about our chalets until it is time for dinner serving. After that it is pub, pub and pub. Then back to someone's chalet for a party afterwards. There would be several parties on the go. There were hundreds of us, and we would not all fit in one Chalet. It was bad enough trying to move about in them when you were living in them never mind partying. Although there were loads of us everyone kind of had their own circle of friends so they would all hang out together or someone would hook the speakers up and we would all party outside. It was just nonstop partying drinking alcohol and taking drugs. There were all kinds of drugs, whatever you wanted you could get it. There were loads of people selling different kinds of drugs. They were supplying them to the staff, the managers and the holiday makers. Everyone knew if they wanted drugs to come to the last row of chalets because that was where all the drug dealers were and that is what Jenna had become. A drug dealer. She was going up and down to Glasgow to get it but now half the staff were taking it. So, she was going back home with more money and more drugs to carry back. We all work long hours, but we party just as hard as we work. We were only eighteen when you are eighteen you think you know everything about everything when in reality you know fuck all. Now there was a guy upstairs from us his name was Dave, he was doing the exact same thing as Jenna, but he was charging double the price. We were stuck out in a complex in the middle of farmland. Ayr was the closest town to us, but nobody knew anyone out here plus none of us could drive. Jenna was getting the bus up and down all the time to go back to Glasgow and fill up with drugs. It was £5 for a gram of speed. It was amazing speed not like the shit you get now. A full gram of speed would keep you awake for 2 full days. This is how good it was. Dave was going backwards and forwards to Glasgow every week, but he was coming back and selling the speed for £10. We were only making £60 a week. If you spent £10 a day on speed you had no money left for anything else plus you would be a day short. The guys were eating living and breathing speed. Half of the waiters and waitresses were on speed. We were the fastest and best load Joan had ever had she said. That was because we were all speeding out our nuts. We looked like walking zombies although our eyes were pinned like dart boards.

We would all give Jenna our money and she would go all the way home and back again so we could all get drugs. I know it was £5 for us and she got it a bit cheaper, but I told her to start charging something extra. We only got one day off a week. Jenna was using hers to go back and forth. It was only fair that she creamed something for herself for all the hassle plus she was the one taking the risk getting the bus back with enough speed to wipe out an elephant. So, she started charging £7.50 she was still cheaper than Dave and word started to spread. People were throwing money at her up front begging her to take their money to get them drugs. Within a couple of months all the staff were practically speeding out their nuts. Nobody had slept for weeks. I used to go back to Jenna and Dee's chalet until it was time to go to bed because I did not want to spend any time with Charlie. I did not need to do this now because we were not sleeping. We were all just constantly speeding out our nuts. That 1 gram of speed that would last us two days was lucky if it were lasting a whole day now because we were constantly taking it.

I think we had gone nearly two whole weeks without sleeping before we took a night off. I do not know how we never collapsed. We were eating speed bombs like smarties. We were taking that much speed that we were having to take more each time to keep us awake because our bodies were getting used to taking it. We had to take a night off the drugs, the drink and the Beachcomber to get a sleep. We did not take any speed during the day and I did not even make the service for dinner. I fell asleep in the chalet after the breakfast serving. Jenna had to go up to the dining hall and tell porky pies saying I had been really sick. I slept through the following day too. So did Jenna. Our bodies must have been knackered. I had stayed awake for two weeks then lost two days sleeping.

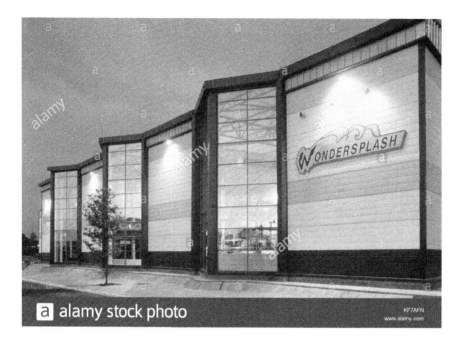

Chapter 8

Jenna had been home to do a drug run. When she got back, she had brought back what looked like two flints out of a lighter. Remember the flints you used to get in the clipper lighters tiny little things. Well this is what she had in her hand. She said that they were acids. I had never tried acid before we were going into Ayr town center for the day. Jenna left first thing in the morning and got back before lunch time. We were going to try this new Chinese for lunch. We took the acid with us and said we would have something to eat first. None of us had ate in days. If you take speed you cannot eat well, I could not eat. The only good thing was I was losing loads of weight between not eating and running about the dining room like a blue arsed fly. Now I needed some new clothes though because everything was too big for me.

We went straight to the restaurant and had lunch. The whole way there all we did was moan we were starving. Everyone on the bus must have been sick fed up listening to us because it was all we said from the minute we got on the bus until we got off. We moaned when we got there that they did not bring the food out quick enough and we were starving. What happened after all that bloody moaning from we left Butlins until the waitress put the food down in front of us, we could not eat it. I think it was just the thought of being hungry. We had not eaten for so long our stomachs must have shrunk. You were lucky if we both had a little bit of dinner and that was it. I asked for a doggy bag. I had just bloody paid over a tenner for something to eat. That could have got me two grams of speed. Too bloody right I was taking it with me. We were going to try the acid so maybe I would be able to eat something later because I was not about to take both at the same time. We took the acid in the Chinese just before we left then headed into Ayr Town Centre.

There we were again moaning. Now we were moaning that nothing was happening. We have just spent £10 on food and not eaten it. Now we have just paid £5 each for an acid and nothing is happening. That was more wages than we make in a day down the toilet pan. All I am thinking is I have just wasted 3 grams of speed. That was 3 days of being up partying all night and I have just wasted it on food I have not ate and an acid that is not working.

We floated in and out the shops looking for new clothes and got nothing. We did not get to do this together on our day off. Sometimes I went home on my day off and Jenna usually used her whole day off to go get drugs for everyone. We were in this shop trying on a 7up matchstick man jumper and I turned round to look at Jenna and her face was melting. Oh, my mother of god all her face was melting like candle wax. I burst out laughing and she asked me what was wrong. Just as I was telling her that her face was melting, she was in stitches. Her acid had started working too. The two of them started working at the same time. She was standing in the middle of the shop and her face was just melting and falling off. She told me I was a marshmallow and my body was all bendy. The two of us were now tripping out our nut in the city center. I was looking at her walking, but it was as if 10 of her were walking at the same time. Each one was a little bit further away than the first one and so on. It was like a Jenna trail. When I put my hands out it was as if it was going in slow motion. We went into a shop and I took a pair of knickers and put them in the bag with my doggy bag when we came out the shop I pulled the knickers out the bag but they were covered in Chinese food and it was as if it was all dripping all over the street. Now everything felt as if it was 100 x slower than it actually was. It is like pressing pause on the tv but then you fast forward in stages. This is how we felt. She was laughing at me. I was laughing at her. We were both standing in the middle of the town center touching each other's hands midair trying to catch them because stuff was dripping all over them. If you were beside us, you would think we have been released from the looney bin for a day and our minder had fucked off and left us. We must have looked like a right pair of idiots.

Then it went from one extent to another, now we are walking about the shops and we think that people are watching us. We think that they are following us about the shops. We are asking people in the middle of the shop why they are following us. We have gone from tripping out our trees to total paranoia within minutes, but it was both at the exact same time. When I was tripping Jenna was tripping now the para is ripping out my arse and hers. I feel as if I am a top service secret fucken spy and

someone from another country is coming after me. Everyone and everything are collateral damage. People are wanting to shoot and kill me for information. Jenna asks me what information and now I think she is on the other side. She is the enemy because she should know what the secret mission is. I am standing in the middle of a clothes shop giving Jenna secret hand movements like we are about to open fire on a village. There is a whole fucken village of people and we are special navy seals who are going to save the fucken world. People are in the clothes shop looking at us thinking who let these two idiots out the funny farm. Have you ever watched a police program and they do all these hand gestures to their squad? This is exactly what we are doing in a fucken clothes shop. They had the cheek to put us out of the shop. Now all hell has broken loose because we have nowhere to hide. In the shop we were hiding behind railings and clothes. Now we are in the middle of the street and I tell Jenna to run because the bombs are coming. We are running up the main road

in the city center screaming at people to run because bombs are coming. Jenna is running with both arms above her head crossed over shouting and I am running behind her. I am surprised the cops did not come and lock us up and throw away the key.

The complex is a bus ride away. It takes about 20 minutes by bus to get back. Now if you are in a car 2 minutes in the car is like half an hour walk. Can you imagine how long a 20-minute bus ride is. Jenna is not getting on the bus. She is telling me there are people on the bus just waiting to kill us. We will need to walk. 20 fucken minutes on the bus is a long ass walk. Can you imagine what a 20-minute bus ride walk is when you are paranoid, and you think everyone, and anyone is out to get you. We were running away from fucken trees. I shit you not. We are running about the streets screaming at the trees. We thought the branches of the trees were extending to come and get us like Venus fly traps. We are running zig zag up the road trying to avoid the tree branches. We are still both screaming at this point. Then it went to the cracks on the pavement. See if you are walking on the pavement and it is like all squares but then you have cracks in the pavement well we thought that if we stood on a crack that the devil was going to open the ground and take us to hell. We have gone from running zig zag up the road to tiny moves in case we stood on a crack. People are walking past us thinking what the fuck. We are screaming at people telling them that they were going to hell because they stood on one of the cracks. We still thought that everybody was out to get us. Let me tell you this it was a long ass trip literally back to the complex. Now the complex is away out in the middle of nowhere. When you actually get to that long stretch of nothingness it is all grassland. If walking on the streets was bad wait to you hear this.

The only way to describe it is all farmland. All you can see for miles is grass and farmland. Now we are not caring about stupid ass cracks on the pavements. Now we are in the middle of the jungle. Jenna says she hears a baby crying and I say it must be Tarzan, us two idiots are running through the grass doing hand gestures to find the monkeys and save Tarzan. See now when I say this back, I think what the fuck but trust me see taking one of those acids fuck me we were wired to the moon. That farmland is a long ass stretch. We searched the whole of that farmland looking for Tarzan. Now when you get to the opening bit of the complex there is security. They are there making sure you are staff, or you have your holiday pass to get in. If you do not have it, you are not getting in and trust me the other option of trying to get what you could say over the fence is a stupid ass idea. It is all barbed wire and a pain in the tits to get in. We have our staff passes. We could have just shown our passes at the front gate but oh no us two idiots think the security men have been put there to catch us and kill us. They are going to hand us over to the other side if they catch us. We still have a mission to do and that is us back to that mission. We are not walking down the grass verge oh no we are on the fucken ground crawling so no one will see us. I cannot begin to describe how fucken far away this was. We had to go all the way down to the beach to get over the barbed wire and wall. It is not easy to get in. That is the way they designed it, so it was not easy to get in for free yet us two idiots are doing the hand gestures crawling among the grass and the reeds to fuck knows where. Now that I think about it, I do not even know where we thought we were going. When we finally got in the place is busy. It is always busy, there were too many people though and the paranoia was still ripping. We both went running back to the chalets. I had made this man like thing in my room out of teddy head and clothes all stuffed with bags. Now this teddy was trying to kill us. Now we know what we have taken but knowing what you have taken and actually feeling what we felt it was the worst god dam afternoon of my life. Jenna said that if we drank orange juice it would help us come off it. Just as we went outside to go get juice we bumped into David and we bought Valium off him and went to our rooms and went to sleep. Never fucken again have I or ever will I take an acid.

Why anyone would want to have that as a drug of their choice is off their fucken heads literally.

I always remember this one story. When we stayed in Sighthill there was a story going about. I am sure it was Pink Floyd the wall acids at the time. They were meant to be lethal. I think any acid will be lethal after that experience. People were taking them and doing really stupid things. Our high rises went 19 floors up and then you can get onto the roof of the flat. That is a long ass way up. Someone took one of they Pink Floyd acids and jumped off the top of the flats thinking they were jumping into a swimming pool. Now I remember clear as day I said that was a load of bullshit. There is no way that can happen, or you can trip out your tree that bad for that to happen but see after my experience with acid. I eat my own words. Anything is possible with one of them and I for one have never touched one again.

Chapter 9

We have been her nearly two months now, I honestly think every staff member was on drugs at this point. The people who did not take it at first were crashing out all the time and missing the partying bit. The shifts were too long or too awkward. All the catering staff did breakfast and dinner. I know it does not sound like much, but you would be in the dining hall for about 7.30am sometimes still drunk but you were there. The chefs and kitchen staff were there at the same time. By the time we had served everyone breakfast then reset our tables it was late morning. Yes, you had a few hours to arse about or do what you wanted to do but then you were back in work doing dinner time and resetting tables, so we did not get finished until late. Our shifts were more awkward than anything else it was split shifts. The red coats however they were fucked. They did get more basic wages, but they were working all day and night. They did not stop until the entertainment stopped at night which would be about 11pm. They had to take drugs or all they would have seen and done was work. I could never understand why everyone wanted to be a red coat. We made more money than them with our tips but then our uniform was the worst. Even the kitchen staff had better uniforms.

Everyone and their granny were taking drugs. It was rife, it was like part of the job description. I am surprised it did not say in the advert staff wanted for Butlins. Must be able to take speed bombs because it is mandatory.

I heard that in previous seasons some people have taken drugs and that drugs were a bit of a problem but now it is a huge problem. If anyone says they were in Butlins working that year and did not touch any drugs I am sure they will be talking shit, but this is the worst year ever.

It is that bad that the Sun newspaper have sent in undercover journalists to find out information and do a story on all the drugs and the police have sent undercover officers in to find out where all the drugs are coming from. You would have a better chance of getting out the crystal maze. Everyone and their granny were taking and selling drugs. It did not just come from one person. This was the problem. This is how they could not nip it in the bud because there were too many sources and far too many people taking them. There were different dealers for drugs one dealer sold speed, another dealer for acid, and one for cannabis or it was a few dealers for each drug.

Have you any idea how many staff there was. We were all doing it. Every row of all the staff quarters had a drug dealer or person who supplied drugs. The managers were on drugs. How the hell do you think they managed to do they long ass hours. We started at 8am and finished at 8pm. Ok there were gaps in between for lunch etc. but you could not go out anywhere after breakfast shift because it was not long then it would be the lunch shift. If we were doing 12 hours how many hours to you think the managers were doing. They did not get a day off. If someone was sick or pulling a sickie, they had to get the shifts covered sometimes they were pulling a 12-hour shift then had to go do another shift. We were all off our faces. It was the only way we could cope with the long hours and have any kind of social life. It got to the point though that we were all taking that many drugs we just did not eat or sleep. I think I went to Butlins a size 10 and came back size 0. The point is it was everywhere. There was not just one dealer so they could find out who is was and shut down the supply link. That was never going to happen because there were too many. Back then it was not like it is now one dealer and everyone else needs to bow down to that one person. They were happy to share. More than one dealer meant it was harder to shut it down. More than one dealer meant one person was not walking about carrying the whole stash. It was not as easy to get caught because not one person knew who all the drug dealers were, but things were about to change.

Chapter 10

It is bad, now we have loads of undercover journalists and cops working with us. They were placed in all different sections. In the dining hall, the kitchen, chefs, red coats and shop staff. There was a mixture of cops and journalists in both. Nobody knew who to trust and who not to trust. It was not like we all started together and finished together. We did all start together, but people dropped like flies. Some people came and they were crying for their mums and went home. Some people came and could not hack the long hours, so they left. Some people came and did not like it. There were loads of reasons but when they people left there was always a backup of staff just waiting to start.

They gave so many people the positions in the beginning but then they had standby staff just waiting for people to drop out. So new people were starting every day. There were chefs, waitresses, kitchen staff, bar staff, amusement staff, food staff, shop staff, gift shops, fair ground. There were hundreds upon hundreds of staff. For it to be a fully functional place we had to be fully staffed always. So, if one went out then one came in and there were plenty of people lined up just waiting to get a job. They were split between every post. We did not have a clue who was who, but it soon worked out in my favour. My lovely roommate Charlie got paired off with a new girl. We were months in, so the new people needed to shadow someone who knew what they were doing. Joan asked if there were people who wanted to volunteer. Of course, she picked herself. That fucker ruined my first experience and now she was just about to burst someone else's bubble. Happy fucken days. Cheerio see you later. I got moved to a chalet of my own. I was happy as a pig in shit. All the journalists and cops could come now for all I cared I got rid of Charlie.

This other new girl started now we knew there were journalists and cops in here. Most of us were 18 we were just barely age to be there and work there. The new girl though was older. Now we did have older people working here. Dee had a friend called Dee Dee. Now she was not really old, but she was older than us. Maybe in her 20's but when you are 18, then being 20 sounds old. Her name was Olivia, she had shoulder length sandy coloured hair. She was an attractive looking woman. She did not need makeup. She was roughly a size 10 and she was taller than Jenna maybe 5foot 8 or 9. She was really softly spoken whereas we were all loud asses in the dining hall. You needed to be for the kitchen. That was the first thing I thought about when I heard her soft voice. How the fuck will she cope in the kitchen. She will look like a timid little mouse.

She did not fit she stuck out like a sore thumb you could just tell

she had I am under cover something written all over her and the funniest thing was she got paired off with Jenna. Of all the bloody people to pair a newbie off with it had to be Jenna. They are in here looking for the people selling drugs and they had just paired one of the cops off with one of the drug dealers. You could not make this shit up. Jenna was clever though. See that little Miss Sandy routine she had that down to a T. That was her ammo, you never in a million years thought it would be her. Now the cop was paired off with her and she was going to shadow Jenna for a few days. She was to work beside Jenna and watch what she was doing, how to serve the food, where to get everything and how to reset your tables again before leaving. This did not stop Jenna taking her speed, she could take it and you would never know she had taken it. She could function the same as normal. She could still eat, and her eyes did not look like pit holes in the snow. If you were shadowing her you would never know she was on it. The rest of us were like cows on roller skates chewing the sides of our faces off talking shit to anyone. This helped us with our tips though. We were all making a packet. Well we had to be to keep buying drugs. Our customers were the happiest ever. Their food would be out like lightening, we would happily do anything they asked us to do. I would give mine extra dinners if they wanted it. There would be a choice of dinners, if they wanted to try one of each, I was more than happy to give them it because I knew at the end of the week it would be a big tip I was getting. The Monday to Friday people were better because they were with you all week and they got to know you. Never once did I not get a tip. I always made big tips, but I always got loads of presents too. I would get presents and cards from the kids or the adults. You might think that it is only five days but five days for breakfast and dinner is a long ass time when you keep giving them extra stuff and talking to them. We would happily tell our customers where to go. The best prices for everything and the cherry on top was their pictures. See that shop with all the photos if any of our holiday makers were in any pictures in the shop me and Jenna would pinch them for them and give them over to them. You know you are getting a big ass tip. If people came back again, they would ask to get put at our tables. Jenna and I would go into the gift shop. We knew the guy in there we would get gifts for our customers free and we would give him a split of our tips. Everybody scratched everyone else's backs to make a quick quid.

We would get free booze at night in the Beachcomber, we were in with the guys behind the bar. We would give them a bung off our tips, or Jenna gave them drugs. It was cheaper for us if she gave them drugs rather than money and I would split the drug money with her. The guy who ran the go karts was in Jenna's pocket. We loved the go karts, but it was the only thing you had to pay for. Anything we wanted Jenna simply swapped it for drugs. There were shit loads of staff so there was more than enough to go round. There could never have been just one person selling drugs. It would have been impossible. The holiday makers who came regularly knew who was selling drugs or where to get them. If you had holiday makers at your tables and you knew they were sound you would tell them where to get the stuff or Jenna would supply, it.

Chapter 11

At first there was only a few new faces, but they seemed to be multiplying. Even although people did drop out like flies and new people replaced them it got to the point no one was leaving but more new people were coming in. We were all fucken raging. There were extra waiters and waitresses this went down like a fucken lead balloon because we got some of our tables taken off of us to share with the newbies. Fuck the newbies. Say we had five tables of twelve then maybe it went down to four tables of twelve. That is like losing three families. That is three lots of tips gone. I never made anything less than £10 off of a family. I always made loads more but that is a bad week. That was at least thirty quid off my wages every week because these new fuckers came. You ask any waiter or waitress we were spitting feather because that was our drug money. You thought it was bad in the kitchen on day one. You should see it now. They were not even arguing and then smashing plates. They were just smashing plates. We gave the kitchen staff and chefs a slice of our tips. It was only fair. That kitchen was like a sauna and they all had long sleeve white coats and hats on. They were sweating like pigs in the butchers. We may all look like enemies on a battlefield in work swearing and throwing shit at each other but as soon as work was finished, we were all best friends again. So, say at our bit where we collected the food there were three or four chefs and say five kitchen staff all of us put money together on a Friday and handed it into the kitchen. This was not compulsory it was out of respect, we wanted to do it. It was only fair. We were all doing the same amount of work but now our tips are being cut so the back hander to the kitchen is cut and now everyone is raging. People were starting arguments over the stupidest of things and throwing plates at each other. I shit you not. If you walked through that kitchen during service, it would be at your own risk and I suggest you wear protective clothing and a hard hat because you will get hit with something. It was like a battlefield not a fucken kitchen. Plates and cutlery would be flying through the air it is no longer a normal word then fuck it is just fuck, fuck, fuck that is it. Chefs screaming at chefs. Chefs screaming at waiters and waitresses. It was a free for all but now we are a cheaper free for all because less money was coming in.

We all hated the newbies. Whether you were undercover or not we fucken hated you because you were taking away our money. It causes a domino effect. None of the other staff got tips. Everyone relied on our tips. We all did it. I am surprised they made any money. The catering staff funded the rest of the staff. Fuck the red coats we never gave them anything except drugs but all the other staff we did because it benefited us. The bar staff, shop staff etc. Our money got cut so we could not hand over as much money anymore so practically the whole of Butlins staff were pissed off and wanted them all out. From then on, all new people got blanked. We did not give a fuck. If they were normal people tough shit. You have come in at the wrong time. All new people were the enemy in all departments except red coats. Fuck them they think they are better than us, but they were useless to us except to the drug dealers. They had nothing to offer us, so they never got a slice of our tips, but every other Tom, Dick and Harry did.

Chapter 12

Our happy go lucky busy complex has now turned into you can cut the tension with a knife. It is like that day Jenna and I took that acid, and everyone was the enemy. This is how the whole place is. We have less money, so the kickbacks are less, and no one has as much money for drugs. They may not have found out who the drug dealers were, but it did slow things down a bit. Until they all came up with a plan to lower the price of drugs for the time being and not to supply anyone new or anyone you did not know. You could not go up to Dave or Jenna and say so and so sent me because they would just tell you to fuck off. Jenna was still getting shadowed by that girl Olivia. She had only been there a few days. She did have her own tables now, but Jenna still had to keep an eye on her and make sure she was ok. Everyone blanked her except Charlie. Little Miss I will tell you everything.

Everyone dropped the price of the drugs for the time being. Any money was better than no money but under no circumstances was anyone to sell anything to someone that they did not know. If they did, they would have blown it for everyone but like I said there were loads of dealers. They all just came to an understanding and things went back to normal, or as normal as they could get under the circumstances. Now we all knew they were in there working. Everyone knew we were already plastered all over the Sun newspaper about all the drug taking and partying. It was a big thing so anyone who dares to say they did not know was talking shite.

Olivia would always try and speak to Jenna, but she would only talk about work and that was it. She wanted to come to the Beachcomber with us, but we never took her. She came up one night when we were there and when she came, we left. We were just trying to get rid of them all as quickly as they came so we could go back to normal. There were no fucken dishes left in the kitchen. We had smashed them all. Joan was doing her nut because she had to keep signing the order for more plates. They would come and we would all smash them again. Out of thousands of plates being smashed there was only one bad accident that I know of because I was there. It was a new girl I cannot even remember her name I am sure she was only there for a few days. She was a pretty little thing. She had a cute wee face and her hair was always in bunches with yellow bobbles. She was softly spoken though, and I remember thinking you will never last here hen. We were all in the kitchen having a plate fight because this is what we used to do. Dodge the plates. Brilliant game but expensive. Two of the chefs were playing dodge the plate and the plate came right in our direction. I do not think she was paying attention and smack right off of her face. She never moved out of the road and the blood just started pouring. I remember trying to put my apron up against it to stop the bleeding and it did not work. As soon as she seen the blood that was her. She was screaming and crying at the same time. Someone went to go and get Joan and I had to take her to the medical place. Bloody great, that was my shift finished so it was now my own time and I got landed with her and had to take her over to medical. Her eye needed stitches so she had to go to Ayr casualty it was the nearest hospital and I had to go with her. I remember thinking I better be back in time to go to the Beachcomber.

Well we were not going anywhere fast. The place was full. It was Saturday night. I think it was about 9pm – 9.30pm when we got there so it was still early, and it was full can you imagine what it would have been like if it was the early hours of the morning. They said to us at the front desk that they were taking priority people first, but they would get to her as quick as they could. I turned around and a guy had just walked in with 2 other men and he had an axe in his face. I shit you not two bigger guys were holding him up. He was a druggie; you could hear it in his voice. He was tall maybe about 6 foot 3 or 4, slender man and half of his teeth were missing. He had a haircut like someone went into the kitchen cupboard took out a cereal bowl stuck it on his head and cut around it. It was a stupid ass haircut. I think the two men holding him up may have been bouncers or security guards. They were not police they had polo shirts on both of them were built like a shit house and both were bald. Really stalky men each one had an arm and they were holding him up. The blood was running down his face and he was chit chatting away as if he was just reading something in the paper. You would not think he was walking about with a fucken axe sticking out his face. I remember thinking well he will get taken before us. Everybody was just looking at him in shock horror and probably wondering the same as me how the fuck are you still ok talking away like nothing has happened, but it was probably the drugs. Not long had he walked in and they took him away.

What a night we had in there it was like watching TV, so many weird and wonderful things had happened. All these people coming in with different stories and most of them were drunk. I missed the Beachcomber that night but in fairness I have to admit I did have a good laugh in Casualty. I swear to god see at the weekend if you have nothing to do and you want a laugh. Take yourself along to Casualty for the night. Free entertainment.

Chapter 13

We have all gone into the dining room as we normally do in the morning, but you can just tell something is not right. Joan and Sammy are standing at the front with other people. Usually they are sprawled all over the tables in the morning. Even though they are managers they still have a life. They hang up Manageress and Supervisor badges the minute they go out. They are two different people. Joan and Sammy the bosses then Joan and Sammy party people. As soon as we went in you could feel it. It was simply weird. As we all started walking down, we were told to stand up at the front. Oh fuck, we are all lined up like skittles waiting to get bowled over. Then a load of police officers came walking up. Me and Jenna just looked at each other. When all this kicked off, she stopped carrying drugs on her and she had a stash place for them. They all did. No one walked about with the drugs on them. We had just taken our speed bomb we had done an all nighter again and I remember thinking Jesus fuck if we get arrested, we are going to be stuck in they bastard cells speeding out our nuts. All the waiters and waitresses were most likely rattling too. We were all in the Beachcomber the night before and then everyone was back at Dee and Jenna's chalet. We all only went back to our own chalets to get changed for work. Drop a speed bomb then up to the dining hall. Now we are all standing here like lambs to the slaughter just waiting to get our throats slashed.

They stood in front of us and then started calling out names. I was just waiting for Jenna and Dave's name to get called. They were the two main waiter and waitress suppliers and they shouted for Charlie. What the fuck did they want with her? Then they shouted Bobby Jo, Ronald and one other guy who I did not know. We were all gob smacked. What the fuck was going on. How come they were shouting from them. I could see Jenna's face she was sniggering. She was most likely thinking thank fuck but why had they shouted the roaster. I wonder what she done.

We did not find out until later. Little miss goby had only gone and grassed herself in. I should have seen that coming. Miss, I want to spoil your experience had only gone and told the undercover cop that she had dropped a speed bomb in the fucken toilet. After all that do not say a word to anyone new. We do not care if you think they are not cops keep your mouth shut. Did she listen? Did she fuck, in fact she is probably in there now singing like a canary. Luckily, Jenna never sold her any speed. I told her not to. I said from day one there was something not right with her. I remember saying if she gets caught with drugs, she will sail you down the Clyde with her. I do not know who sold her the drugs but whoever it was they would now be sitting in the cell next to her. Even we did not know everyone selling drugs as I said there were loads of

them. That is why they could not shut it down. If there was only one supplier, it would have been shut down ages ago.

The other people that got taken away the same time as Charlie were in her circle of friends or someone that she knew of. I do not know if we whistled or they just randomly took them with her but there were police officers everywhere. The chalets got stripped and searched looking for drugs. They were all taken away by police car to the police station. We never saw any of them again. God knows what happened to them, but they did not come back to work. Normal service resumed after that. There were still police officers and journalists working amongst us, but I think after the first gun ho everyone kept their mouth shut after that.

These are all my memories of Butlins although Butlins was not just about me and my experience it was everyone else's experience. This was thirty odd years ago and still everyone from Butlins is on a Butlins page on Facebook and they go to reunions. If you have a look on the page you would think they were all still there. I could not write a book and not involve everyone else because it was their experience too and by God did, we all enjoy it.

I have contacted people of Facebook to say what they enjoyed most about Butlins or their personal experience. I am not changing their words. I will simply write it up the same way they tell me because that it exactly what my books are about. People just saying it like it is. I hope you enjoyed my experience and now you can read what everyone else thought.

Everyone who worked in Butlins through the years' Experience

Caroline McDonald – worked there from 1990/1992

They were the best days of my life. Butlins made me the person I am today. I Live life to the full now. I remember a lot of good friends who have now become my second family. There was a lot and I mean a lot of great parties and had to be knocked up every morning for work. Oh, how I wish we could go back to those days, life was so much simpler and carefree.

Donna Shannon – worked there from 1989 - 19992

It is where I met my family thirty odd years later, we are all still family and friends for life.

Allison Knox – worked there from 1990/1991

Right, I am Allison Knox, I worked as a waitress in 90/91 they were the best days of my life and memories of my Butlins family that I will cherish forever. Ok I am going to sound like the bitch of the book but you swept all the rubbish up from the canteen and put it on my chairs (I have spoken to Allison about this – I do not remember it and I have apologised) I can remember it was someone's birthday and they had a party at Hollywood Studios in Glasgow and there was a bus that took us there and back. The song they were playing on the bus was that song – Oh sit down James. I used to do all the wee drawings on the place mats – we stole them out of the dining room. I was in tick all week for my medicine until Sunday when it was pay day.

Lorraine Fraser – worked there from 1985/1988

That was the year the police were everywhere they were all over camp. A little boy went missing from one of the chalets. The police searched all the staff chalets and visitor chalets looking for the little boy. There were hundreds of people, police and sniffer dogs out looking for him. He was found weeks later up the hills. That same year a young boy drowned also. Good luck with the book, we all have many a story about Butlins and what we got up to. We all have great memories. It would be great to go back to the old camp Stuart Ballroom. I worked there 85/88 and it was 1988 the little boy went missing

Jim Patterson – worked there 1984/1986

I am Jim Patterson – worked in the bars in 84/85/86 mostly the Beachcomber – to all the staff that I worked with in those years you have made me proud to have known you all.

Chris Dawson – worked there 1990/1992

I worked in Main catering in Ayr – It was the best days of my life – 30 years on and we are still best friends – they are the best friends I ever had

George Hall – worked there 1995/1998

I also worked the first season when it was Haven – I worked in security

Hugh Brown – worked there 1976 then came back 1984/86

I worked there in the boating lake and the amusement park – I worked there before your time but then I came back again – A good load of old times to be had – You should get plenty good stories

Joseph Scott – I have no clue what year

Well Butlins was like joining the nunnery and I led a sheltered life compared to my colleagues who thought it was a holiday camp to party all the time, we did have to get chapped up for work though.

Marie McCrum – Worked there 87/88

Liz Murray – Worked there 1987

Jim Jack – Worked there 1985/87

I worked as a waiter in main catering -oft what a time we had – the picture he sent was outside the pool after staff talent contest

Tony Clarke – worked there 1988/89

I was a waiter, diet chef and I also worked in the go karts – I have lots of stories from hiding cutlery because there was never enough to go around so it was better to hide it for your own tables – I ran a night time hit squad (tying up the newbies to a tree naked because they just started) I was there the year the little boy disappeared and was unfortunately found dead. We wll looked for him – I cannot remember all the details just that we all looked for him and it was very sad. We had chocolate cake fights with the waiters and waitresses and also the customers – the cake was called death by chocolate It all started when I fell onto the tray of cake I was carrying, I then hit another waiter for laughing – which in turn kicked it all off. – We had loads of friends getting clothes, cigarettes, alcohol and food for free was just part of being in the staff club – you would go into the clothes shop run by Butlins – go in try on whatever you liked and walked out the shop with it – we would go to the bar all night and drink for free – you never paid for anything – all my wages packets piled up in the top drawer of my staff accommodation D6 til I go to a posh supervisor chalet – TV and wood paneling instead of woodchip – Sometimes the TV's would get robbed just after they left – I was not part of this but I did hear about it – I was so drunk one night on my way home I fell into a different chalet – climbed into bed – fell fast asleep and then to be woken up by the two owners who just laughed because luckily they knew me

Tony Clarke – Chalet D6

Kevin Boyle – worked there

Hi Debbie, well done writing a book about Butlins and the staff – I am Kevin Boyle – I worked in Butlins for a long time and I was the lifeguard. It was the year Butlins was all over the papers when the little boy drowned 😥 such a sad story – Butlins and the staff were admonished from all charges of neglect to the boys well being in the pool – I do not know if you remember that – I was offered a new start and job as a way of thank you from Butlins and I transferred into security and then along came the missing boy story – but to this day I still think about the staff and their kindness to come together in strength to help the police look for the little boy. There will be lots of stories some good, some funny and some sad. I loved my time in Butlins – Kevin Boyle

Paul Burke worked there 1994/98

I also worked at Haven 1999 – I was the manager in the photo shop (I am surprised you actually sold any all the staff stole them lol) - sorry xxx

Colin Scougall – worked there 1990's

I performed there as a cabaret act in the 1990's. The band was Davy Halford on keyboards – and a drummer – we played in the Showboat which was bursting at the seams and the atmosphere was electric – On one occasion I was an opening act for Buck's Fizz. Happy Days – When I played there it was still chalets which were steeped in History

Jane Robertson (Maiden name Rae)

She met Colin whilst working there – lots of fun and happy memories of our time there – I worked in the pizza place whilst Colin worked in pickwicks - when we left we moved in together and went on to have 4 boys. Sadly Colin passed away 2016 -the memories that we had was of pay day – we would get up and go and get our wages and head into town – go for something to eat – get some shopping then head to Rabbies for a couple of Shandies (aye right) before heading back to camp – we got the cheapest fags you could get (Black Cat) on our first date Colin took me to the Bakery on site for a glass of milk and a donut lol – Heinz was in charge of retail catering. Made a lot of good friends that I keep in contact with -I just wish we could go back in time – I would not change a thing – best days of my life

James Livingston – Worked there 1980/86

We were the main band in the Stuart Ballroom – in 1980 our first year we did Thursday nights only – in the Continental Bar we drove 100 miles to do the gig and back again for the full season – in 1981 we started our first season playing six nights a week – plus Saturday morning saying goodbye to the campers. – I also got involved in other things happening on camp like doing a challenge match every week for 6 years with pro snooker resident

Jim Medowcroft

A comedy routine then on a Thursday night afternoon 5 a side on the roller rink with Roy Aitken or Bobby Lennox. All great times – All great until last year 2019 when we lost my great pal (Gerald Griffin) aka Gerry the tramp – sadly missed as is my pal Jim Meadowcraft – I went to both funerals after a lifetime of friendship

Susan Glancy – Worked there in 1977

I worked in 77 in the coffee bar Stuart Ballroom – I had went there with my cousin but she hated it and she went home – I had a chalet to myself that was great until nearing the end of season – I got back to my chalet to find a very big woman sitting on my bed – I said oh who are you and she said I am Lizzy fae Easterhoose I am your new roommate – Jeezo Lizzy was not very clean and she gave me the fear 💀 to cut a long story short she went way out one night and came home really drunk and singing Koomba Ah – Next day in work I told my friends and them made arrangements to go out and leave Lizzy in – I was so relaxed when I went out but when I went back to the chalet to get back in Lizzy shouted get to fuck I am getting shagged – I stayed with my friends and the next day Lizzy got kicked off the site – when I got back to the chalet she had stolen all the towels and toiletries and left a note saying – See you, ya wee cow face I will find you and knock your heed aff – even to this day – I still watch my back for big Lizzy fae Easterhoose.

Eddie McGrath – worked there 1987

I made £45 a week – it was the best job ever – I would not have swapped it for a grand a week – the stories though – ooft not for sensitive eyes and ears – dozens ended up in Slough after the season 87 and some are still there – the benefits were outstanding – I moved beds into chalets – emptied the bins at night etc. – Think I was a porter although I did do some waiting on occasions when old Frank got really desperate – I also remember a death on a roller coaster and then pretending to punters a wheel fell off – there was a bank robber there using his job as an alibi – gang bangs – countless sex stories – countless sackings and rehiring – wrecking chalets every night – 30 waiters walked out in one day – and the same number moving to Slough at the end to continue the buckfast party 😊 xx

Carol Anne Mooney – worked there 1989/90

I worked there in 89 I worked in the cashiers – I met my husband there back in 1990 – he was in retail catering – a catering assistant in Sept he became retail supervisor – got married weekend of the country and western weekend in 1991 – I was in main catering my husband was a cook – that was my last season because I was expecting the first of my Butlins babies – Our marriage did not make it – we divorced in 2011 – defo great memories though – I would do it all again in a heartbeat – apart from getting married lol xxx

Jane Walker – worked there 1991

Went to Butlins a quiet shy person nobody thought I would make it on my own – I always spent my time with my mum and mu Aunt – mostly my Aunt though I did have loads of friends – I was a homebody My brother in laws sister Lorraine was coming down the day after me to start – she did come down but she did not last long and she went back home again to be with her ex-boyfriend – they had a daughter together and they stayed together until sadly he passed away – I went there on my own – I was not scared – I was looking forward to it – I worked in main catering – I was a waitress – I loved all the hustle and bustle – I am the kind of person that likes to keep busy – It was really funny in the kitchen – we all used to fight and shout with each other – there would be all out war over tea pots and cutlery – Now when I think back about it – it was hilarious – I met a lot of good friends but Debbie was my bestie – she was a wee red headed fire cracker – crazy as shit but I loved her and got to know her – as I soon found out I was like her – it just took me leaving home to realise how strong a person I was – I shared a chalet with a girl called Donna – she had dark hair and I got on well with her too – I absolutely loved the party life – I hardly slept the whole time I was there – I just could not do it anymore – I am pushing 50 – when I knew I had enough of the party life in Butlins – I called my aunt and uncle to come and get me – I packed all my stuff and went back home – Debbie and I stayed in touch for years afterwards and then life took over and we lost each other but now we have found each other again – I am never going to let the little fire cracker go

Debbie Ross – worked there 1991

I had the best time ever – I was only there for one season – Only one other person said it and I cannot believe it because fucken cutlery was like gold if you worked in the dining room – that and plates – Cowboying other people's tables – this was a must – you could hire a TV for £10 a week I think it was but no one watched TV – I do not think anyone sat about long enough to watch TV – I am surprised Butlins did not go bust – none of the staff paid for anything – we got paid our wages every Sunday – we had no dig money to hand in – all our meals were free – anything from any of the shops were free and we did not pay for booze either - £62 does not sound like a lot but remember this was 30 bloody years ago – it was a lot of money back then – Nobody got themselves up for work – all the supervisors from every department knocked the doors in the morning to get the staff up – I hardly slept – I did not want to sleep and miss anything – The only thing you did need to pay for was the launderette they fuckers couldn't be bought or give freebies so we all washed our clothes in the baths. – we lived like kings and queens – if you did not take drugs then you could not spend your money. If you went there for a whole season and did not buy drugs you would have come home loaded – even fags were free depending who was on – I really do not know how it managed to stay afloat – we all robbed the place blind – it was like part and parcel of the position – and everyone did it – if you say that you did not you are talking shit – we all scammed – every single one of us – It was the best job I ever had and the most fun – so many amazing memories that will stay with me forever.

To Wrap shit up

All the comments and messages from other people who worked there are in their own words. This is how I like to write – As far as I am concerned say what you want and how you want – A lot of the words are Scottish slang but fuck it – they are staying as they are.

I have tried to put as many of your pics in as I can - If you read the messages or speak to anyone who worked in Butlins they all say that they had the time of their life – Not one person who lasted a season has said it was shit because it was not – It was the best job ever – I will never have as many memories from one job as I have from Butlins – It was only fair to let other people have their say and send in their pictures – we all experienced it together – some longer than others – It is just hard to explain as a job – I hope I have done it justice because it really was one big party – Obviously my memories and experiences will be different from other peoples but I have written it my way – I have explained it my way – Thank you to all the people that I met through this wonderful journey – I had an amazing time and I would not change a thing – maybe just remember more but I have written what I remember from my time there.

I want to thank two ladies in particular Jane Walker and Donna Shannon – no matter what happens we will always be in each other's lives – I love both of you and I am so glad we found each other again after all this time

I am just an ordinary girl telling stories. I write them the same way I would tell them. There are no fancy words or perfect grammar in my books. I call a spade a spade in real life and that is the exact same way I write. If you are looking for a book with perfect grammar that describes how blue the sky is and the shapes of the clouds. You will not like my books. I get straight to the point if I was on TV half of it would be bleeped out. This is how I write. It is most definitely not for children. If you are the kind of who does not have a stick stuck up your arse you will like my books. I do a mixture of novels and short stories - some will be funny - some will be sad - I hope you enjoy reading them. Thanks for stopping by - If you have read any of my books and want to leave comments good or bad I will take what you guys say onboard or if you prefer the funny ones rather than sad or vice versa. I will try mix it up a bit

Other Books - Novels

Drunken Stories

Growing up in Sighthill

Pay Back is a Bitch

Butlins Wonderwest in Ayr - The True Butlins

Short Stories

Fuck you Landlord

Knickers for Rent

A night on ecstasy

What an expensive night out that was

Book Night

Make your own fucken way home

These are all available on Amazon under Debbie Ross

Printed in Great Britain
by Amazon

81948605R00051